W9-AAZ-175

ISBN 0-7683-2094-1

Written and Illustrated by Flavia Weedn
Foreword by Lisa Weedn
© Weedn Family Trust
www.flavia.com
All rights reserved

Published in 1999 by Cedco Publishing Company
100 Pelican Way, San Rafael, California 94901
For a free catalog of other Cedco® products, please write
to the address above, or visit our website: www.cedco.com

Library of Congress Cataloging-in-Publication Data

Weedn. Flavia.
    The prize: a collection of stories / written & illustrated by Flavia Weedn.
        p. cm.
    ISBN 0-7683-2094-1
    I. Title.
PS3573.E2895P7 1999
811'.54--dc21   99-12114
                                                               CIP

Printed in Hong Kong

1 3 5 7 9 10 8 6 4 2

No part of this book may be reproduced in any manner without written permission
except in the case of reprints in the context of reviews.

The artwork for each picture is digitally mastered using acrylic on canvas.

*With love and gratitude to those talented souls who made this book a reality—
Rick Weedn, Lisa Mansfield, Diana Musacchio, Jane Durand, Tyler Tomblin,
Heather Day, Solveig Chandler, Hui-Ying Ting-Bornfreund and Annette Berlin.*

A COLLECTION OF STORIES

The Prize

Written and Illustrated by Flavia Weedn

Foreword by Lisa Weedn

Cedco Publishing Company • San Rafael, California

Dedicated
to R. J.

TABLE OF CONTENTS

FOREWORD

Some people are gifted with a sense of rare beauty. They cradle life like they would a delicate feather. They treat it gently, revel in its imperfect splendor, stand in awe of its miracle, and through their abiding faith they transform a single quill into wings on which to fly.

My mother, Flavia, is such a person. Even her name is poetry.

As a child, I recall being aware of Mama's ability to always make us feel uniquely blessed. When other mothers filled crystal vases with carefully manicured roses, or wallpapered their dining rooms with the latest in home decor, mine planted geraniums in coffee cans and tied ribbons around them — ribbons that matched the color of some leaf pattern in a faded vintage pillow, or of the chipped paint on a well-worn chair that she had rescued from a thrift shop. "Nothing is more beautiful than that which has been touched and loved and part of a dream," she'd say.

While her peers attended parties and social events, Mama would invite the neighborhood children to come sit on the floor of her studio and listen to her tell stories as she painted. They'd watch her blend color into magic and were captivated by her every word. She provided a place where secrets were safe, where none were judged, and where every soul felt a sense of belonging.

As time went by, young and old alike gathered around Mama to listen to her tales of wonder and insight. Her magic was touchable. It still is.

Mama has a way of making those around her believe that something very wonderful is about to happen. "Watch closely," says she, "and listen with your heart, for there is always music to be heard."

Today, as a woman, I feel a deep sense of pride as I behold my mother's grace. Her wisdom, born of hope and eternal faith in the human spirit, is revealed in her divine simplicity — a quality I now recognize as the profound courage of a spirit unafraid to be.

The Prize is a collection of stories written by a rich soul: a woman blessed with an awareness of life we are all free to own. Woven of truth and sprinkled with lessons she's learned along the way, her tales awaken us all to life's music.

Feel the magic.

– Lisa Weedn

A Lifetime

I remember reading in school
about some great
historical figure
who spent a lifetime
seeking his fortune.

And about a famous
somebody else
who spent a lifetime
doing good deeds.

So when I was ten
I thought a lifetime
meant the length of time
spent on years
from birth 'til death.

That its value was measured
by the important things
that happened
during those years.

And the only valuable
lifetimes
were those found
in library books.

When I was twenty
    I was impatient with life
    and with time
    so most of my days
    slipped by unnoticed.

    I reached out for tomorrows
    trying to catch a glimpse
    or a touch
    of what my lifetime
    might bring.

I found by my thirtieth year
    that life had brought me pain
    but mingled with it
    was all the joy I'd found.

    Life had been kind
    to me
    for it had not
    left me
    untouched.

A part of me
thought my lifetime
was spent.
The rest of me
kept pushing
for what most surely
would happen
tomorrow.

But that was then.

Today I looked at tidepools
and seabirds
and found an ageless rock
washed smooth and gray
by the sea.

I sat on the sand
with my friend
and shared thoughts
and tuna sandwiches
and the sun.

I gave corn chips
to a seagull
and watched him smile.

My friend and I walked
and talked
and looked
at people
and into
store windows.

We saw beautiful birds
in handmade cages
and I remembered
the seagull.

My friend told me
of faraway places
and we laughed
and bought Christmas tree
ornaments.

I listened closely
to the words of a song
that he sang
about a poem
written on the back
of a leaf
and about a key
to a house
with no door.

At a street corner
we shared
the discovery
of a flower
growing
deep inside
a drain.

Souvenirs, all.

When I was ten
how could I have known
that a lifetime
has nothing to do
with years . . .
only with time.

And that its value
isn't measured by
the important things
that happen . . .
unless smiling
with a seagull
is important.

A lifetime?

I spent one
today
with my friend.

❧

The Playground

I saw a playground
   today
   deserted and empty
   except for one old man.

   He sat very still
   and to some
   he would have been
   unnoticed.

To the left of the swings
stood a freestanding
sculpture
made for children
to climb on.

But it was so perfectly
perfect
I suspected it would
have been happier
somewhere else.

The sun was so warm
and so bright
it played tricks
through the leaves.

It made me want to run
and hang by my knees
on the bars
and hide
in the tunnel
and pretend.

It was early afternoon
and children
belonged there.

I sat on the grass
and wondered why
the sight
of an empty playground
bothered me so.

The old man
     had not moved
     since I first saw him.
With bent back
     he just sat on the bench
     and stared into space.

He looked so very alone
     my heart remembered
     a part of a poem
     about the last leaf
     upon a tree.

He turned his head slightly
but enough
and I could see
he was smiling
and he wasn't alone
at all.

His old friends were there
young again
running
and shouting
playing
and pretending.

He was out there
playing among them
young like they
and filling each moment
with something new.

All of them
were laughing
and playing at life
like a game.

Spellbound
I watched
as the playground
became older
and different.
The magic
I was seeing
was all for free.

I heard the squeaking
    of swings
    and the scuffling
    of feet.
    The children were all
    around me
    so close
    we could touch.

    The sounds in
    the playground
    grew louder
    and my eyes flashed
    from the old man
    to the children
    then back again
    to the sun
    in the trees.

Suddenly
the old man
stood up
and my symphony
was over
as abruptly
as it had begun.

I watched him
pick up his cane
and slowly
walk away.

It was I
who was motionless
now and alone
and the only sound
in the playground
was the pounding
of my heart.

I looked
at the fallen leaves
that had scattered
around me
and those still clinging
to the trees.

I was strong
with the feeling
that I had stepped
into someone else's
dream.

As he walked away
the old man
never looked back.
Not once.
But there was no need.
He knew.

His friends
would be there
waiting
in the playground
whenever
he needed them.

Twigs

The calendar
claimed November
but summer
had designed the day.
We drove
along the coast
my mother
and I.
Both marveling
at the people
who could steal time
from Wednesdays
to sit on the beach.

Maybe it was the magic
of the California sun
or the surfers
or the hot dog signs
but an hour later
as we walked
along the sidewalks
even the store windows
and the city signs
couldn't make me think
of anything beyond
how golden and how warm
the day.

But once we had
entered the store
and closed
the big wooden door
behind us. . .quite abruptly
all signs of summer
had disappeared.

Strangely and suddenly
we were standing
in a world
filled with Christmas.

The air
was actually
a winter's chill
and heavy with the scent
of pine and of maple
of cinnamon sticks
and the earthly potpourri
smells of Christmas.

Christmas trees
    stood tall and proud.
    Each one
    reaching
    for the high wooden beams
    of the ceiling.
    Each one
    heavily adorned
    with bangles and beads
    wooden figures
    fabric fancies
    tiny toys
    and silver bells.

    Each one
    selling Christmas.

The glass ornaments
made twinkling rainbows
on the walls
and the shines
and shadows
made each tree aware
as they competed
in their silent beauty pageant.

The hum of people's
conversations
mixed together
with the sounds
of many footsteps.
Decisions of what to buy
for whom
were overshadowed
by the beauty
that engulfed the room.

My mother and I
became a part
of the crowd.
Very like
everyone else.
A little lost
in the magic
of the room
and in our own
personal reflections
of Christmases past.

When we left the store
and walked to the car
we each carried
one of the store's
white printed bags.
Each filled with remnants
of the Christmas we'd found.

Inside mine
carefully wrapped
in tissue
was a gift for her.
And in my mother's
a gift for me.

On the quiet ride back
we relaxed.
My mother mentioned
how hot
the late afternoon sun.

I noticed
the stragglers
lingering
on the beach.

As the road turned
away from the coast
toward home
the eucalyptus trees
appeared
on our right.

The silhouettes
of their blue-gray forms
stood in all their glory
against the burnt-orange
of the sky.

But . . .
up close
their shapes seemed
tired and old
like forgotten people
standing
lonely
in
an
empty
field.

I stopped the car
   when we saw
   the piles of dried
   branches and boughs
   that had fallen
   from the trees.

   They lay still
   as they beckoned through
   the patterned streaks
   of sunshine
   that spread over them
   on the ground.

We began
   to gather
   great bunches
   of twigs . . .
   my mother and I.

Two women
   ankle deep
   in broken leaves
   and branches.

Two women
   stumbling
   and giggling
   in soft smooth dirt
   by the side
   of a busy highway
   filling our arms
   and then the trunk
   of the car
   with dusty twigs.

Time eluded us.

We were
children again
as we stepped over
and reached through
and laughed
while bits of
the twigs
we gathered
clung to our clothing.

While
   we loaded the car
   we spoke
   of wrapping
   bunches of twigs
   with giant cloth ribbons
   and giving them
   as Christmas gifts . . .

   gifts of
   gathered firewood
   to burn
   on Christmas Eve.

Whatever
Christmastime
magic
that each of us
personally
felt as children
had returned.

I watched
my mother's face
and saw
how her eyes
belied her age
as they
smiled back
at me.

I felt
a surge of warmth
within me
when I realized
that for those
few moments
in time
we had managed
to melt years away.

We were
    as two young friends
    sharing
    the spontaneity
    of a rare
    and beautiful
    experience . . .

    and without
    opening
    any store tissue
    or printed paper bags
    we were exchanging
    gifts with each other.

We had found
Christmas . . .
my mother and I.

Not in that shiny store
but here and now
in this field.

And these gifts
to each other
we would keep
forever . . .
for they were not found
in the twigs . . .

but in the gathering.

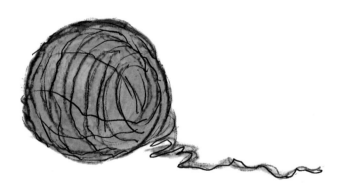

Sometimes

Sometimes
   she comes to me
   when my head
   is already so full
   I think
   my mind
   can't handle
   another thought.

   Then simply
   by her presence
   she has a way
   of fading away
   the heavy stuff.

Maybe that's why
she chooses
those times
to come to me.
Or do I
choose
those times
to let her in?

Is she my escape?

She took much with her
when she first went away.

Sometimes
I think she took
more than she left
behind.

Her disappearance
was slow
and gradual
and now
I suspect
no one ever sees her
but me.

I've given away
some of what she gave me
to my children.

They
who never knew her
share her sensitivity
her vulnerability
and her deep love
of being.

Her most personal things
I've kept for myself . . .
some leftover dreams
and a handful
of hopes
that died too young.

Sometimes
I can see clearly
the print of her
high school
graduation dress.

Or hear
the Hoagie Carmichael
song
that was playing
the first time
she fell in love.

I can remember
        sometimes
        the foolish things
        she used to do
        and now
        they make me
        smile.

        And the warm times
        when she and I
        are very alone
        together
        and I realize
        how easy it is
        for her
        to make me
        cry.

Most of my days
are very crowded now
and I forever hurry.
Even my time shared
with her
is hurried.

But it's time
I need
for it is necessary
to look back
and touch her
sometimes
just so she can see
where I am going.

There are times
   she seems just beyond
   my sight
   and I can only imagine
   the look
   of her face
   of her hands . . .

   and the pure
   and beautiful
   UNCOMPLICATEDNESS
   of her life.

I wonder
    if she knows
    how much
    I miss her . . .

    sometimes . . .

    this girl
    that I used to be.

∞

The Gift

Someone stole my car
   last night.
Damn!
How could they?
I feel empty.
No, more than that
I feel offended
and violated
and angry.

Kind:
  VW Karmann Ghia
Year:
  1967
  Old.
Color:
  Faded gold
  Earl Scheib gold.
Plates:
  WBL 226
  Pronounced wobble.

  Had original black plates
  original tool kit
  even original owner's manual.
  Nifty, I thought,
  but nobody asked

Identification marks:
   None I could list.
   All the marks I could
   think of
   were those
   no one would understand.

   Case number:
   512-183
   The investigating officer
   left his card.
   It read *Sheriff-Coroner.*

   Coroner.
   How appropriate.
   This is a eulogy
   for a Karmann Ghia.

If whoever took it
    doesn't rub Armor All
    on the dashboard
    the leather will crack.
Karmann Ghias do that
    you know.
There's some
    in the glove compartment
    with my cologne.

How stupid!
My car's been stolen
    and I'm staring out my window
    hoping the thief
    will take care
    of the dashboard.

For almost seven months
   I've lived in a small
   beach house
   whose main source of light
   comes from shuttered windows
   which overlook
   a narrow strip
   of parking
   which overlooks
   a wider strip of sand
   which the ocean overlooks.

   Most of these months
   I've spent alone
   or so I thought
   until I realized
   I wasn't.
   I had someone.

   I had me.

Old habits faded
new ones were born.
Began keeping
my car and house locked.
Even bought one of those
chain things
for my door.

My car was always parked
in the same place
under the street light
first space
from the corner.
The one
that's empty now.
Exactly twelve
steps from car to house.

I know, I counted.
It's one of the
new habits
I had developed.

So there my car has been
every night
parked and locked
just where it belonged.

Then, last night
someone came
and took it.

Its predecessor
had been a new Porsche 911.
Expensive and impressive
fully equipped
ski rack and all.
Gorgeously dressed
in its elegant original
Porsche Desert Tan creation.

No scars
no signs of wear
only wax
and gloss.

When I drove the Porsche
I felt wealthy.
Dollar wealthy.
Like the world
was looking
at me.

I justified my soul
with repeated tales
of why
I deserved to own it.

My life had already begun
to change
when the Porsche
was sold.
And I felt good
about selling it.
I would be free
of the built-in guilt
that was slowly surfacing.

Guilt that came
from owning something
I truly felt
extravagant.

And so . . .
three months ago
I bought
my ten-year-old
Karmann Ghia.
Found it on a dirty
and dusty vacant lot.

I knew it would become
part of my plan
to simplify my life.
A part of my change
of direction
and search
for peace of mind.

If there had ever been
a doubt
in my head
whether or not
this car was right
for me . . .
it disappeared
when I realized
it had no reverse gear.

Significant
you see
because
now
I could
only
go
forward.

It had the look
of a classic
waiting
to be rescued.

Not a superstar classic
like Katharine Hepburn
more of an
Irene Dunne.

They don't make them
anymore
you see
so it was like
finding a rare book
one out of print.

I liked the feeling.

What else
did I leave in the car . . .
that research I'd done
on children's books.
A sketch pad or two.
Some drawings.
Proof sheets
of Christmas cards.
Lisa's shoes
the straw ones.
A box of Kleenex
white.
My sun glasses
and a Bic pen
fine line.

Oh Lord, something HAS died.
I've just listed
the last effects.

I must get things
   into perspective now
   and stop making
   such a big thing
   out of this.
   Cars are stolen all the time.
   It's not like
   losing a loved one.
   It's only a car.
   A material thing.
   Something
   that can be replaced.

   But . . . it was a loved thing
   and how can I replace
   all that I feel for it.

And tell me . . .
how can I replace
my gold bracelet
in the side pocket
or the belt
to my burgundy dress
that temporarily
had become the latch
that held up the back seat
or the Indian blanket
in the back window.

The old faded one
I carried Kookie in
the last time I took her
to the vet.

The very last time.

It's not right . . . it's not!
I want it back!
Why did they choose
my car anyway?
They could see
it had a mushed-in nose
and there was no tape deck
no speakers.
Just an AM radio
and a clock
that didn't run.

It's dark now.
As I close my shutters
my parking place
is still empty
save for a tossed beer bottle
which, to the delight
of my sense of justice,
shows no reflection
from the street light.
All this about a car.
How ridiculously sentimental
for allowing myself
to become so attached
to a machine.

There must be
something good
to come from this.
Somewhere a hidden gift
a lesson learned.

Maybe when my anger
subsides
and I have more time
to think about it
I'll know what it is.

And maybe then I'll realize
that nothing can ever
be replaced.
Ever.
Because people
and things
and feelings
don't replace
each other.

They were never meant to.

Each new thing
that comes into our lives
becomes a part of us
and adds to
what we already are
and to what we already feel.

That's the gift
isn't it.
Realized now
at this very moment.
All the love I felt
for everything
in and about that car
are feelings
I still have.
Feelings that are
a part of me . . .
a part of what I am.
My car was never
anything but a car.

And a car was all they took.
They couldn't take away
my feelings.

Oh Lord,
   by some special miracle
   let me see a car
   parked on that empty
   parking place
   tomorrow morning.
   An ordinary car
   Earl Scheib in color.

   Let it be there
   just long enough
   for me to say thank you . . .
   and to tell it that
   I still have
   all the gifts
   it gave me.

∞

The Prize

There's this man
    that I know
    who makes me think
    deep thoughts
    about myself.

It's not that he asks.
He never has.
He doesn't say it
with words.

But there's a look
in his eyes
and a way
that he smiles
that makes me
ask myself
questions inside.

It's as if
he's learned secrets
that very few know
or holds the key
to some wisdom
he's found.

This same look is shared
by others
I've met
and I know
each has found it
alone.

It's not money
or power
or position
he holds . . .
he just celebrates
being alive.

The merchants
    on the streets
    who sell their souls
    and the frightened ones
    who hide inside
    could change their lives
    if they had what he has
    but they stay
    on their
    merry-go-rides.

    I think
    he feels guilty
    sometimes
    for the way that he lives
    his contentment
    just to be
    and to feel.

Yet inside he knows
it's the world
that he owns
and all that he has
is for free.

Like the feel
of the sand
on the beach
when it's warm
and the nights
when he touches
the sky
and when the songs
that he finds
and keeps giving away
come back
as a memory.

It's not really a secret
you see
that he's found.
It's something
each of us has.

It gets lost
sometimes
or just covered up
or we think
someone
takes it
away.

So I'll hold on
to the thoughts
that he's made me think
and I'll be unafraid
to grow.

For that's step one
and the first thing
to learn
if I want to be
all I can be.

I'll never know
   all the thoughts
   of this man
   this friend
   who touched my life.

   Because
   one day
   he'll
   just
   go away
   and I'll never
   see him
   again.

But he touched my mind
and I know
deep inside
that I now
own the truths
that he's found.

That TO LIVE
is the game
and I've already won . . .

because LIFE
life itself

is the PRIZE.

∞

Other Flavia Books

Forever: Footprints on Our Hearts

Across the Porch from God: Reflections of Gratitude

Across the Porch from God: A Gratitude Journal

To Take Away the Hurt: Insights to Healing

To Take Away the Hurt: A Healing Journal

Heart and Soul: A Personal Tale of Love and Romance

Heaven and Earth: A Journal of Dreams and Awakenings

Blessings of Motherhood: A Journal of Love

Dear Little One: A Memory Book of Baby's First Year

Passages: A Woman's Personal Journey

Photo by Chris Chandler

Flavia

Flavia Weedn is one of America's leading
inspirational writers and illustrators. She
encourages the expression of real feelings, while
portraying the basic excitement, simplicity and
beauty she sees in the ordinary.

Flavia's concern to bring hope to the human
spirit constitutes the core of her life's work. For
over three decades, she has touched the lives of
millions through books, cards, fine stationery
products, posters, and hundreds of licensed
goods throughout the world.

Flavia lives in Santa Barbara, California.